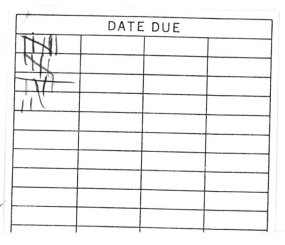

MICE ON MY MIND

BY BERNARD WABER

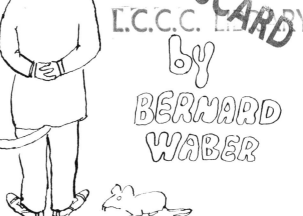

HOUGHTON MIFFLIN COMPANY, BOSTON, 1977

For some friends on my mind:
Irma, Richard, Val and Ted

Library of Congress Cataloging in Publication Data

Waber, Bernard.
 Mice on my mind.

 SUMMARY: It is impossible for Cat to think of any-
thing but mice, mice, and more mice.
 [1. Cats — Fiction. 2. Mice — Fiction] I. Title
  PZ7.W113Mi   [E]   77-9050
 ISBN 0-395-25935-5

Do you want to know something?
I've got mice on my mind.
Mice! Mice! Mice!

I go to bed each night.
What do I dream about?
Mice! Mice! Mice!

I wake up each morning.
What do I think about?
Mice! Mice! Mice!

I try so hard
not to think about mice.
I take cold showers.

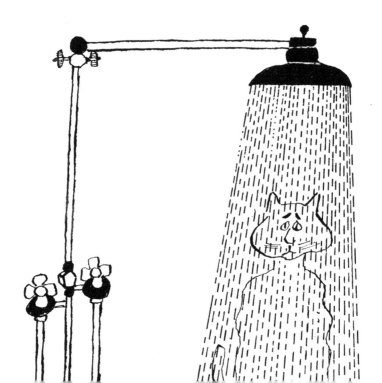

I soak in hot tubs.

I jog.

I practice deep-breathing exercises.
Breathing in — uhhhhhhhhhh!
Breathing out — huuuuuuuuuuh!
Wishing there were mice about.
Mice! Mice! Mice!

I thought having a hobby would help.
I took up needlepoint.
But this is what I made.

I tried my hand at painting.
These are samples of my work.

I read books.

I wrote poetry.

"High on a hilltop
in a little wooden house
something was scurrying
mayhap it was a _ _ _ _ _"

I switched to word puzzles.

"What five-letter word,

for small rodent,

begins with M

and ends with E?

Hmmmmmmmmmmmmmm..."

I thought perhaps I should
be getting about more.
I went to the opera.

I dropped in on friends.
What do you suppose everyone talked about?
Mice! Mice! Mice!

It isn't as if I haven't
tried to catch a mouse . . . or two . . .
or three . . . or four . . . or more.
Oh, how I have tried!
I turned my place into a dream house for mice.
I scattered cheese everywhere.

I drilled inviting little holes
into the woodwork.

I dimmed the lights,
built a roaring fire,
played sweet music.

I even pretended I wasn't home,
as I waited for
Mice! Mice! Mice!

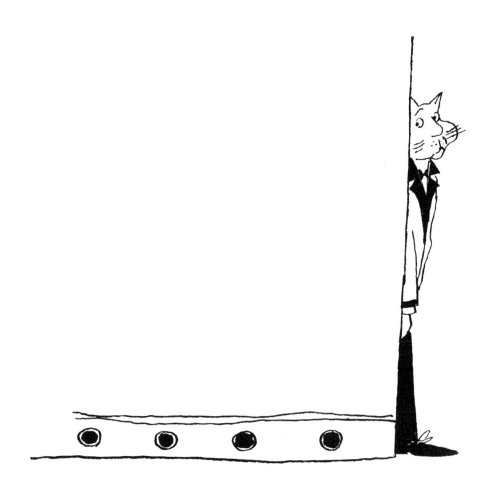

What do you suppose happened?
I'll tell you what happened.
Nothing happened —
except now, my house smells of cheese.
And I'm stuck with all these
drafty little holes in the woodwork.

It's so unfair.
I don't know why
this should be happening to me.
I've been good all my life —
never an unkind word for anyone.
I pay my taxes.

I'm nice to children.

I give at the office.

I donate my blood.

I ask for so little . . .
just a little mouse.

I think I deserve a mouse.

I can't remember when last I saw a mouse.
Was it weeks ago?
Was it months?
Was it years?
Was it ever?
Do I believe in mice?
Are there really mice?

You would think, in this day and age,
if one desperately desired a mouse,
one could simply pick up the phone
and Dial-A-Mouse.

In the good old days we had mice.
Believe me, mice were no problem.
Nobody went without.
Everyone had mice.
That's the trouble with
the way things are run today.

I think I'll write a letter to the President.
I'll say:
"Dear Mr. President,
Bring back the good old days.
Bring back
Mice! Mice! Mice!"

Do you want to know something?

It's getting to me.

It's really getting to me.

I'm not at all well.

I keep seeing beady little spots

before my eyes.

And for weeks now, I've been hearing

strange, scratching sounds.

DOCTOR'S OFFICE

I went to the doctor.

I said, "Doctor, I need help."

He said, "What is your problem?"

I said, "Mice! Mice! Mice!"

He said, "So. Tell me more."

I said,   "Every night I dream about mice.
           Big mice, little mice, fat mice, skinny mice!"
He said,   "How interesting! Tell me more."

I said, "Gray mice, black mice, white mice, blue mice,
          orange mice, green mice, yellow mice, purple mice,
          striped mice, polka-dot mice, rainbow mice!"

He said, "Delightful! Tell me more."

I said,   "Running mice, jumping mice, hopping mice,
                 skipping mice, dancing mice, twirling mice,
                 tumbling mice, cartwheeling mice, handspringing mice,
                 spinning mice, swimming mice, bobbing mice,
                 floating mice, flute-playing mice, flying mice!"
He said,   "Stupendous! Tell me more!"

I said,   "Country mice, city mice, sleeping mice, waking mice,
            nice mice, bad mice, sad mice, gay mice,
            talking mice, laughing mice, mincing mice, silly mice,
            sneering mice, snickering mice, simpering mice,
            snarling mice, rascally mice!"
He said,   "How thrilling! Tell me more!"

I said,   "Millions and billions and trillions of
             Mice! Mice! Mice!"
He said,   "Tell me more!
             Tell me more!
             Oh, please, tell me more!"

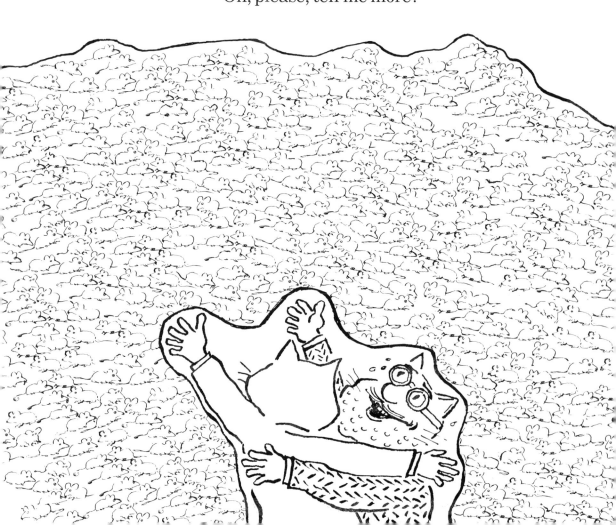

I said, "Doctor, I have to get out of here!
I have to go out and find myself some
Mice! Mice! Mice!"

He said, "Wait! Wait! Wait!
I'll go with you!
I'll go with you!
I'll go with you!"

I stopped seeing that doctor.
Do you want to know something?
I could be wrong, but I think
he has the same problem.

Well, I thought I had lost hope
of ever finding mice.
But today I came across this interesting
little item in the newspaper.

It says here how the folks
in Upper Transpopolis are having
a problem with mice.
It says here how the entire country
is overrun with mice.

Now isn't that a shame.

Heh, heh, heh.

Perhaps I can lend a helping hand.

What am I waiting for!

UPPER TRANSPOPOLIS HERE I COME!

Wish me luck.